Two of the Best

Eleanor Robins

High Noon Books
Novato, California

Cover Design: Jill Zwicky
Interior Illustrations: Rick Hackney

International Standard Book Number: 1-57128-181-9

9 8 7 6 5 4 3 2 1 0
0 9 8 7 6 5 4 3 2 1

Contents

CHAPTER 1

Best on the Team

It was the first day of volleyball practice. Gwen could hardly wait for practice to start.

Last year Gwen had been named the best player on the school team. This year she hoped to be the best again. And she hoped to make the All Area team.

School wasn't over for the day. It was only lunch time. Gwen met Eve in the lunch room. They had lunch the same period.

Eve was Gwen's best friend. Last year they

had both been on the volleyball team.

They quickly got their food and sat down. They always ate lunch quickly. Then they talked the rest of the period. They always had a lot to talk about.

"Did you find out anything?" Gwen asked.

"Yes. Did you?" Eve answered.

"Yes. What did you find out?" Gwen asked.

But Jake walked over to their table. And Eve didn't get to tell her right then.

Jake was in Gwen and Eve's science class.

"You know how to do that homework for science?" Jake asked Gwen.

"Yes. Why?" Gwen asked.

"I need some help with it. Is it OK for me to

call you for some help?" Jake asked.

Gwen said, "Sure. But call tonight. I have volleyball practice this afternoon."

"You going out for that again this year?" Jake asked.

Eve said, "She sure is. Gwen is the best player on the team. She might even make the All Area team this year."

"Maybe I'll see you play," Jake said.

A boy called to him. He went over to the boy's table and sat down.

"I think he kind of likes you," Eve said.

Gwen said, "I think he just wants help on science. Now tell me. What did you find out?"

Both girls wanted to know who was going

out for volleyball.

"The girls on the team last year are trying out again. Also, five new girls," Eve said.

Gwen said, "I heard six."

"Some of the girls who quit last year will be at the try outs," Eve said.

Those were the girls who had quit because they didn't make the starting team.

Eve said, "Second team is OK. But I sure wish I could make the starting team this year."

"I hope you do, too. It will be more fun with you on the starting team," Gwen said.

"I'm going to wish for our team to be No. 1. Wouldn't that be great?" Eve said.

"It sure would be. But don't get your hopes

up," Gwen said.

Gwen wished they could be No. 1, too. But she didn't think they had a chance to be. They would need another very good player. Gwen knew all the other girls going out for the team. None of them played that well.

Gwen looked at her watch. "We have to go. See you later at practice."

CHAPTER 2

Great News?

School was over for the day. Gwen hurried to the gym. She could hardly wait for volleyball practice to start.

Eve ran into the gym. She was almost late. She looked excited. She quickly went over to Gwen.

"I have some great news," Eve said.

"What?" Gwen asked.

Then Coach Carr said, "Quiet, girls. My turn to talk. Your turn to listen."

All the girls quit talking.

Coach Carr said, "I'm glad to see all of you. I know most of you from last year. We should have a good team this year."

All the girls yelled, "Yes! Yes!"

Coach Carr looked over at Gwen. Then she said, "We might even have someone make the All Area team this year."

That made Gwen feel very good.

"You girls need to work hard to play volleyball well. We'll work on skills a lot. We'll run in place a lot. Any questions?" Coach Carr said. No one had a question.

Coach Carr said, "First, we'll run in place. Then we'll do stretching exercises."

They ran in place for a while. Then Coach Carr showed them some stretching exercises. Then they practiced passing the ball.

Later Coach Carr showed the new players how to serve. Gwen and Eve had time to talk.

"What's the great news?" Gwen asked.

"We have a new girl in my math class. Her name is Pam. She just moved here. She started school today," Eve said.

"Why is that great news?" Gwen asked.

"Last year Pam played volleyball. She was voted the best player on her school team," Eve said.

Gwen was surprised. "I don't see her at practice," she said.

Eve said, "She couldn't come today. She didn't know we had practice. So she didn't tell her mom she would be late. But she'll be here tomorrow."

"Coach Carr might not let her join the team late," Gwen said.

"I took Pam to meet Coach Carr after our math class. She said it was OK for Pam to come late," Eve said.

Gwen knew she should be glad the team would have another good player. But she wasn't so sure she was glad. Last year she had been the best on the team.

This year she might not be the best.

CHAPTER 3

The New Player

It was the next afternoon. Gwen was on her way to practice.

Eve called to her. "Gwen, wait up."

Gwen stopped and turned around. Eve had a girl with her. They walked quickly to Gwen.

Eve said, "This is my best friend, Gwen. Gwen is the best player on our volleyball team."

"I'm glad to meet you. I haven't met many people here yet. I'm very excited about meeting all the players," Pam said.

"I'm glad to meet you," Pam said.

"Where do you live?" Gwen asked.

Eve answered for Pam. "Pam lives next door to Jake."

"Do you know Jake?" Pam asked.

Eve laughed. Then she said, "Oh, yes, Gwen knows Jake. He kind of likes her. He's always asking her for help with his science homework."

"Is he your boy friend?" Pam asked Gwen.

Gwen said, "No, he's not. And he doesn't like me. He just wants my help with science."

They hurried into the gym.

Coach Carr said, "Girls, this is Pam Hall. She has just moved here. She was on her school volleyball team last year. And she was named the best player. Welcome to our team, Pam."

The other girls went over to meet Pam. Then it was time to start practice.

They ran in place for a while. Then they did stretching exercises.

Coach Carr showed some of the new girls how to serve. She showed them how to spike and how to block.

All of the girls practiced their serves. Then they tried to spike and block.

Gwen could see that Pam knew how to play. But she couldn't tell yet how good a player Pam was.

Coach Carr said, "It's time for practice to be over. So we have to stop."

It had been a long practice. The girls were

tired. Most of them were ready to stop.

Coach Carr said, "Tomorrow we will have teams and play some games. I want to find out how ready you are to play. And how well you play as part of a team."

Gwen always liked it when they did that. Her team had always won last year. Yet the same girls hadn't been on her team each time.

"Bye, Gwen. See you tomorrow," Pam said.

Pam seemed nice. Gwen wondered how good a player she was. Was Pam as good as Gwen or maybe even better?

CHAPTER 4

Two Teams

The next afternoon Gwen hurried to volleyball practice. She always liked to go to practice. Today they would have teams and play some games.

The girls jogged in place for a while. After that they did some stretching exercises. Then they practiced passing for a few minutes.

Coach Carr said, "Time to play some games. Gwen, you be on one team. Pam, you be on the other."

Then the coach told five girls to be on Gwen's team. Next she told five girls to be on Pam's team. Eve was on Gwen's team.

Pam's team won the coin toss. Pam served first. Her overhand serve was a good one. It hit on Gwen's side of the court. Pam's team got the first point.

Pam's second serve went so fast that it hit the court, too.

Gwen's teammate hit the third serve back. But it landed outside the court. Pam's team had 3. Gwen's team had 0.

Gwen was surprised that Pam was such a good server.

It was still Pam's turn to serve. Pam hit an

underhand serve. The ball went so fast that it landed on the court. Pam's team won six points before Gwen's team got to serve.

Gwen served first for her team. She served well. But her team won only three points.

Then it was time for Pam's team to serve again. Both teams played very hard.

The score was 14-9. Pam's team was ahead. Both Gwen and Pam were in the front row.

Pam's teammate served. It was a good serve but not a great one.

Eve set the ball for Gwen. Gwen spiked the ball. But Pam was able to block it. The ball fell to the court on Gwen's side. Pam's team got a point. And Pam's team had won the game 15-9.

"Good game, girls. We will take a short timeout. Then we'll play another game. Same teams," Coach Carr said.

Later they played two more games. Gwen's team won the second game 15-12. But Pam's team won the third game 15-11.

The games had not been fun for Gwen. Pam was a very good player. Gwen knew Pam might even be a better player than she was.

CHAPTER 5

Player of the Week

For the next two weeks the girls worked hard at practice. Pam seemed to get better and better. But Gwen wasn't sure that *she* did. Maybe I'm trying too hard, she thought.

It was the day before the first match. After practice Coach Carr put two lists on the wall. One list had the starting team on it. The other list had the second team on it.

Gwen was on the starting team. So was Pam. Eve was on the second team.

"I'm sorry, Eve. I wanted you to be on the starting team with me," Gwen said.

Eve didn't seem to be upset. "That's OK. I'm really not that good. I'm just glad to be on the second team."

Gwen was excited. She was even more excited the next night. It was time for the first game to start. Gwen's team won the serve toss. Gwen served first.

Gwen's first serve wasn't hit back. Her team was off to a good start. Gwen served well. Later in the game Pam served well, too.

Both girls played well when others on their team were serving.

At times Gwen would set the ball for Pam.

The team was off to a good start.

And Pam would spike it over. At other times Pam would set the ball for Gwen. And Gwen would spike it over.

They played hard. Their team won the match. It was a team win. Gwen and Pam had played very well together. They had helped the team. They had helped each other.

Jake walked over to Gwen after the match. He said, "You play OK."

"Thanks," Gwen said.

"Want to go out with me sometime?" he asked.

Gwen was surprised. She said, "Maybe. After volleyball is over for the year."

Maybe Eve had been right about Jake.

Maybe he did like her after all. But did she like him? Gwen wasn't sure what the answer to that question was.

Three nights later the team had its second match. They won again. Again Gwen and Pam played well together. They helped each other.

Gwen and Pam were getting ready to go home after the second match. Coach Carr called to them. They walked over to find out what she wanted.

Coach Carr said, "The two of you played great this week in both matches. I'm sure one of you will be the Area 5 player of the week. But I hope they name both of you. Then they will have co-players of the week."

"When will we find out?" Pam asked. She looked excited.

"Tuesday morning," Coach Carr said.

Gwen could hardly wait to find out who was player of the week. She thought Tuesday would never come.

Coach Carr had told her to come by after science. Gwen could hardly wait for science to be over.

Eve stayed to talk to the teacher. Gwen hurried to the gym as fast as she could.

She was almost to the gym door. She could see a big note next to the gym door. Had she been named player of the week? Or had only Pam been named?

Gwen quickly read the note. There was only one player of the week. And she wasn't the one. It was Pam!

Slowly Gwen walked to the lunch room. She got her food and sat down. But she didn't want to eat.

She saw Eve come in. Eve hurried over to Gwen. She said, "I guess you know."

"Oh, yes. I know."

Eve said, "I'm sorry, Gwen. I thought you were the best."

"Thanks. But your vote doesn't count," Gwen said.

"But look on the bright side, Gwen. Maybe you'll be player of the week next week," Eve told her with a smile.

That didn't make Gwen feel any better.

Eve went to get her food. Then she came back and sat down with Gwen. "Are you OK, Gwen?" she asked.

"Sure," Gwen said.

But Gwen wasn't OK.

CHAPTER 6

You Can't Quit!

That afternoon Gwen didn't feel any better. She didn't want to go to volleyball practice. But she knew she had to go. She had never wanted to miss practice before.

The girls were all around Pam. They told Pam it was great that she was player of the week. They told her she was the best. Gwen wished they had said that to her.

Gwen thought she had played as well as Pam. Co-players of the week should have been named. Or else someone from another school should have been named and not just Pam.

Gwen was no longer the best player on the team. She was just one of the two best. But she wasn't even sure she was still that. Gwen was feeling very sorry for herself.

"Time for our first game. So get ready," Coach Carr said.

The starting team played the second team.

Gwen served first. She hit the ball too hard. It hit outside of the court.

"Don't hit it so hard next time," Coach Carr said.

Gwen served again. It wasn't a very good serve. It did stay in the court. But her team didn't get a point.

Soon it was Pam's turn to serve. Her first serve was a very good one.

"Great serve, Pam," Coach Carr said.

Gwen knew the serve had been a great one. So did Pam and the other girls. So why did Coach Carr have to say it was?

Later Gwen and Pam were both on the front row. Pam set the ball for Gwen. Gwen tried to spike the ball. But she hit the net.

Coach Carr said, "You hit the net, Gwen. Be careful next time you spike."

Gwen knew she had hit the net. So did the others. Coach Carr didn't have to say she did.

On the next serve the ball fell between Gwen

and Pam. But it was closer to Gwen. She didn't hit it. No one else hit it.

"Sorry, Gwen. I thought you were going to hit it," Pam said.

"Next time one of you needs to call for the ball," Coach Carr said.

But they all knew Gwen should have hit it.

A few minutes later she forgot she had just hit the ball. And she hit it two times in a row.

Coach Carr said, "Gwen, keep your mind on what you're doing."

Gwen thought practice would never end. She had never played that badly at practice before.

That night Gwen called Eve.

"I'm going to quit the team," Gwen said.

"You're going to quit?" Eve almost yelled at her.

"Yes," Gwen said.

"Why?" Eve said not as loudly as before.

"You heard Coach Carr this afternoon. She didn't think I did anything right," Gwen said.

"You know that's not true, Gwen. She only said something to you three or four times. She said something to the rest of us, too. You are still upset because you didn't make player of the week," Eve said.

"That isn't why," Gwen said.

But Gwen knew that really was why. Pam was best player of the week. And Gwen wasn't. Pam didn't ever seem to do anything wrong.

"You can't quit, Gwen," Eve said.

"Yes, I can," Gwen said.

"No, you can't," Eve said. She was almost yelling again.

"Yes, I can. My mind is made up," Gwen said.

"You have to stay on the team," Eve said.

"I don't have to do anything," Gwen said.

"Please," Eve said.

"No," Gwen said.

Eve said, "You are thinking only about yourself. Think about our team. We might have a chance to be No. 1 in Area 5."

"Maybe you'll still have a chance. You'll still have Pam on the team," Gwen said.

"But we might have a chance to go to the state play-offs this year. We can't make it there without you. You have to play," Eve said.

"Without me you'll have a chance to play on the first team," Gwen said.

"I don't care. I would rather be on the second team of a good team. And not the first team of a bad team," Eve said.

Gwen wished she could feel good about being second best.

"Don't quit yet, Gwen. Say you'll think about it," Eve said.

"OK," Gwen said. But she didn't think she would change her mind.

CHAPTER 7

No. 1

Gwen thought a lot about what Eve had said. And she didn't quit the team.

Gwen tried to be more like Eve. She tried not to worry about being the best on the team. She just tried to play the best she could. She tried to be happy for Pam when Pam played well.

The team won almost every one of their matches. Pam was named player of the week one other time. But Gwen was also named player of the week two times. There was a good chance their team would be No. 1 in Area 5.

The girls were very excited. They could hardly wait for the play-offs.

It was the last game of the play-offs. The girls had won their play-off matches.

The team that won the game would be No. 1. Gwen's team was ahead 14-13.

Eve was playing. It was Eve's turn to serve. Gwen and Pam were on the front row.

Eve hit an underhand serve. The ball went over the net by only a few inches. The other team easily hit it back.

A teammate passed the ball to Gwen. Gwen set the ball for Pam. Pam spiked the ball. A girl tried to block it but she couldn't. The ball hit the

35

court on the other side.

Gwen's team won the game 15-13. They had won the play-offs. They were No. 1 in Area 5. The girls yelled and yelled.

Gwen and Pam had both played great in the play-offs. Which one would be named best player of the play-offs?

Gwen hoped so much that she would be the one who was named.

"Good luck, Gwen," Eve said to her. Gwen could hardly wait. And then it was time to find out.

One of the officials said, "Quiet please so everyone can hear me. The best player of the play-off games is Pam Hall."

Gwen knew Pam should have won. But Gwen felt she should have won, too. They had both played well in the play-offs.

The officials should have named two best players. But they never did that.

Gwen made herself smile. She didn't want anyone to know how bad she felt.

CHAPTER 8

Two of the Best

Monday at school the big win was all that people talked about.

After school the team had practice for the state play-offs. The girls were excited.

Coach Carr said, "I'm proud of all of you girls. You all worked very hard. But we still have to work hard this week. We have a very good chance to be No. 1 in the state."

The girls started to yell loudly. Coach Carr waved for them to be quiet.

Then Coach Carr said, "Gwen and Pam, see me in my office. Everyone else, practice some on your passing."

Gwen and Pam went into the gym office with Coach Carr.

Coach Carr said, "Both of you played great in the area play-offs. I'm very proud of both of you. You worked very hard. And you always tried to do your best."

"Thanks," both girls said at the same time.

Gwen could tell Coach Carr had something else to say to them. Something she didn't want the other girls to hear. Gwen wondered what it might be.

Coach Carr said, "Both of you should be

named to the All Area team."

That made Gwen feel very good.

But then Coach Carr said, "Two players from the same school could be named. But two have never been named before. I'm not sure they will do that this year."

Gwen no longer felt good. She was sure Pam would be the one to make it. Pam had already been named best player of the Area 5 play-off games.

"I'm sure one of you will be named. But I don't know which one. I don't want the other to be upset. Just remember that you both played well. I'm sure the other will be named to the second team," Coach Carr said.

Gwen wanted badly to be named to the first team. But second team would be better than nothing.

"When will you find out?" Pam asked.

Coach Carr said, "Tomorrow morning. Now let's get out there and get busy. We have to get ready for the state play-offs."

It was hard for Gwen to wait. But at last the next morning came.

Gwen was excited. Soon she would know who had made the All Area team. But she was already sure it would be Pam and not her.

Gwen went to the gym after first period.

"Have you heard yet, Coach Carr? Gwen asked.

"Not yet, Gwen," Coach Carr said.

Gwen went to the gym after second period.

"Did you get a call?" Gwen asked.

"Yes, I did," Coach Carr said.

"So who made the team?" Gwen asked. But she was almost afraid to hear the answer.

Coach Carr said, "Sorry, Gwen. It was only a call about the time of the state games."

Gwen went to the gym after third period.

Pam was already there. She could tell that Pam had made the team. She started to turn around and go.

Coach Carr called to her, "Gwen, great news. You made the team. You and Pam both." The coach was very excited.

*"You both have been named
to the All Area Team."*

She said, "For the first time ever two players from the same school made the team. Our school doesn't have just one. We have two of the best players in our area."

Gwen was so happy that she couldn't say anything. She had met her goal. She had wanted to make the All Area team, and she had!

Her team had a chance to win the state play-offs! Maybe Gwen had a chance to make the All State team, too.

Gwen was very glad that she had not quit the team. She kind of hoped Jake would be there cheering in the state play-offs.